D0340062

play forever on video and

DISNEY DVD

© Disney

Published by Ladybird Books Ltd.
A Penguin Company
Penguin Books Ltd., 80 Strand, London WC2R 0RL
Penguin Books Australia Ltd., Camberwell, Victoria, Australia
Penguin Books (NZ) Ltd., Private Bag 102902, NSMC, Auckland,
New Zealand

10 9
Printed in Italy

Walt Disney's

CLASSIC

THE Lion King

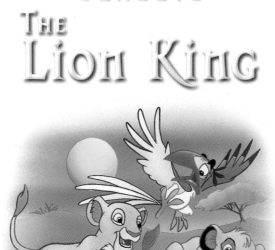

Ladybird

As the morning sun rose high over the African plain, animals and birds gathered eagerly at the foot of Pride Rock.

"There he is!" one of them cried suddenly. "There's the new Prince!" At once everyone cheered and stamped their feet. "Welcome!" they shouted. "Welcome, Prince Simba!"

They watched in silence as Rafiki, a wise old baboon, raised the lion cub high in the air. The clouds parted and the sun's rays shone down on the future King. Slowly Rafiki lowered his arms and took Simba back to his proud parents, King Mufasa and Queen Sarabi.

It was a very special day.

Time passed quickly for little Simba. There was so much to learn. One morning the King showed his son round the kingdom. "Remember," Mufasa warned, "a good king must respect all creatures, for we exist together in the great Circle of Life."

Later that day Simba met his uncle, Scar. The little cub proudly announced that he had seen the whole of his future kingdom.

"Even beyond the northern border?" Scar asked slyly.

"Well, no," said Simba sadly. "My father has forbidden me to go there."

"Quite right," said Scar. "Only the *bravest* lions go there. An elephant graveyard is no place for a young prince."

Simba hurried away to find his best friend, a young lioness called Nala.  Even though he knew it was wrong, Simba had decided to visit the elephant graveyard with Nala that very day.

He had no idea that Scar had ordered three hyenas to go to the elephant graveyard too. Scar wanted them to kill the cub as the first step in his plan to take over Mufasa's kingdom.

Simba raced ahead across the plains, leading Nala to the forbidden place. Eventually they reached a pile of bones and Simba knew they had arrived. "It's creepy here," said Nala, "where are we?"

"This is the elephant graveyard!" Simba
cried. He was about to explore a skull
when he saw Zazu, his father's adviser.

"You must leave here *immediately*!"
Zazu commanded. "You are in great
danger."

But it was already too late! They were
trapped. Three drooling hyenas had
surrounded them, laughing menacingly.

Simba took a deep breath and tried to roar – but only a squeaky rumble came out. The hyenas laughed hysterically.

Simba took another deep breath.

ROAARR! The three hyenas looked round into the eyes of – King Mufasa.

The hyenas fled howling into the mist.

Mufasa sent Nala and Zazu ahead and walked slowly home with his son. "Simba, I'm very disappointed in you. You disobeyed me and put yourself and others in great danger."

Simba felt terrible. "I was only trying to be brave like you," he tried to explain.

"Being brave doesn't mean you go looking for trouble," said the King gently.

The moon shone brightly above them and the stars twinkled in the dark sky.

Mufasa stopped. "Look at the stars! From there the great kings of the past look down on us. Just remember that they'll always be there to guide you, and so will I."

Simba nodded. "I'll remember."

Meanwhile Scar had devised another plan to get rid of Mufasa and Simba.

Next day Scar led Simba to the bottom of a gorge and told him to wait for his father. Then the hyenas started a stampede among a herd of wildebeest, rushing them through the gorge towards Simba.

At that moment Mufasa was walking along a ridge with Zazu. "Simba!" he cried. "I'm coming!"

The King raced down the gorge and
rescued his son, but he could not save
himself. He fell backwards onto an
overhanging rock as the wildebeest swept
by him. Looking up he saw his brother.
"Scar, help me!" he cried. But Scar
just leaned over and whispered,
"Long live the King!" Then
he pushed Mufasa into
the path of the
trampling wildebeest.

When the stampede was over, Simba ran
along the gorge to his father's side.
"Father," he whimpered, nuzzling
Mufasa's mane. But the King did not
reply, and Simba started sobbing.

"Simba," said Scar coldly, "what have you
done? This is all *your* fault," he lied. "The
King is dead and you must *never* show
your face in the pride again. Run away
and never return."

As Scar returned to take the royal throne
at Pride Rock for himself, Simba stumbled
exhausted and frightened through the
grasslands towards the jungle. He took a
few more shaky steps and collapsed.
Hungry vultures circled above him.

Eventually Simba opened his eyes. A warthog, called Pumbaa, and Timon, a meerkat, were gazing down at him. They gently poured water into his dry mouth.

"You nearly died," said Pumbaa. "We saved you."

"Thanks for your help," said Simba, "but it doesn't matter. I've nowhere to go."

"Why not stay with us?" said Timon, kindly. "Put your past behind you. Remember! *Hakuna matata* – no worries! That's the way we live."

Simba thought for a moment and decided to stay in the jungle with his new friends.

Many years later, deep in a cave, Rafiki stared at a picture of a lion. "It is time," he said, smiling, and prepared to leave.

The very next day Simba rescued Pumbaa from a hungry lioness – it was Nala! The two friends were delighted to see each other again. Nala told Simba about Scar's reign of terror at Pride Rock and begged him to return. "With you alive, Scar has no right to the throne," she said.

"I can't go back. I'm not fit to be a king," Simba said sadly.

"You could be," Nala told him.

Simba showed Nala his favourite places
in the jungle. "It's beautiful," she said.
"I can see why you like it – but it's not your
home. You're hiding from the future." She
turned and left her friend alone.

That night Simba lay by a stream thinking. He heard a noise and looked up.

"Come with me," said Rafiki. "I will take you to your father."

Simba followed him in wonder and disbelief to the edge of the stream. As Simba looked into the water, his reflection gradually changed shape and became his father's! Then he heard Mufasa's voice: "Simba. You must take your place in the Circle of Life. You are my son and the one true King." Then the reflection and Rafiki disappeared.

Back at Pride Rock, the rains had been late coming and the land was parched. The hyenas paced impatiently round King Scar. "We're starving," they howled. "The herds have gone. There's nothing to eat."

Storm clouds gathered in the distance and a lightning bolt scorched the earth. As the dry grasses caught fire, huge flames swept towards Pride Rock. A lion appeared through the smoke. It was Simba!

Scar lunged at Simba determined to kill him just as he had Mufasa. In the fierce battle that followed, Simba finally heaved Scar over the cliff face. Scar called to the hyenas to save him, but Nala and the lionesses drove them back. Simba was victorious!

Nala went to Simba's side. "Welcome home!" she whispered.

As they smiled at each other, it started to rain. The heavy drops soaked the dry ground and streambeds filled up once more. The plains came back to life and the herds returned.

One dawn
the animals
and birds
made their
way again to
the foot of
Pride Rock.
Watched by the
lions, Pumbaa and Timon, Rafiki picked
up a tiny cub. He showed the new
Prince – the son of King Simba and Queen
Nala – to the cheering crowd below.

That night Simba watched
the stars rise in
the sky.
"Everything's
all right, Father,"
he said softly.
"You see, I
remembered."
And the stars
seemed to
twinkle
in reply.

Yours
to own
on ᴅɪꜱɴᴇʏ
DVD

WALT DISNEY

CLASSICS

Magical stories t